Dedications

For my Grandma Betty, Grandma Darling, and Tūtū Lilia
Kimo

To Renee, for all of your love, patience, and support
Scott

ISLAND HERITAGE™
PUBLISHING
A DIVISION OF THE MADDEN CORPORATION

94-411 Kō'aki Street, Waipahu, Hawai'i 96797-2806
Orders: (800) 468-2800
Information: (808) 564-8800
Fax: (808) 564-8877
islandheritage.com

ISBN NO. 0-93154-864-0
First Edition, Twenty-second Printing , 2015

COP 142912

Limu

The Blue Turtle and His Hawaiian Garden

Written by Kimo Armitage
Illustrated by Scott Kaneshiro

ISLAND HERITAGE™
PUBLISHING

Limu the Blue Turtle had the most beautiful underwater garden in the entire ocean. It was so beautiful that sea creatures came from faraway places to live there.

Limu loved his colorful Hawaiian garden and took very good care of it.

One day, Limu saw his friend Jonah, the humpback whale. "Aloha, Jonah!" he yelled.

"Aloha, Limu!" replied the whale. "I know you love beautiful things, so I brought you a beautiful seaweed tree from the Faraway-Forest."

"Thank you so much! I love it!" said Limu.

Limu planted the seaweed tree in his underwater garden.
It looked beautiful among his other seaweed and corals.

The seaweed tree grew and grew.

It grew so big that it blocked the sun from the other seaweed trees and they started to wilt. When there was no more seaweed to eat, the small fishes left. When there were no small fishes, the big fishes had no food, so they left.

Soon, there was nothing in Limu's underwater garden
except the huge seaweed tree.

Limu decided to take the seaweed
tree back to the Faraway-Forest. Even
though this seaweed tree was beautiful, it was
not good for his Hawaiian underwater garden.

He put the seaweed tree in his mouth and started swimming towards the Faraway-Forest. The tree was very large. It seemed to grow heavier and heavier with each paddle.

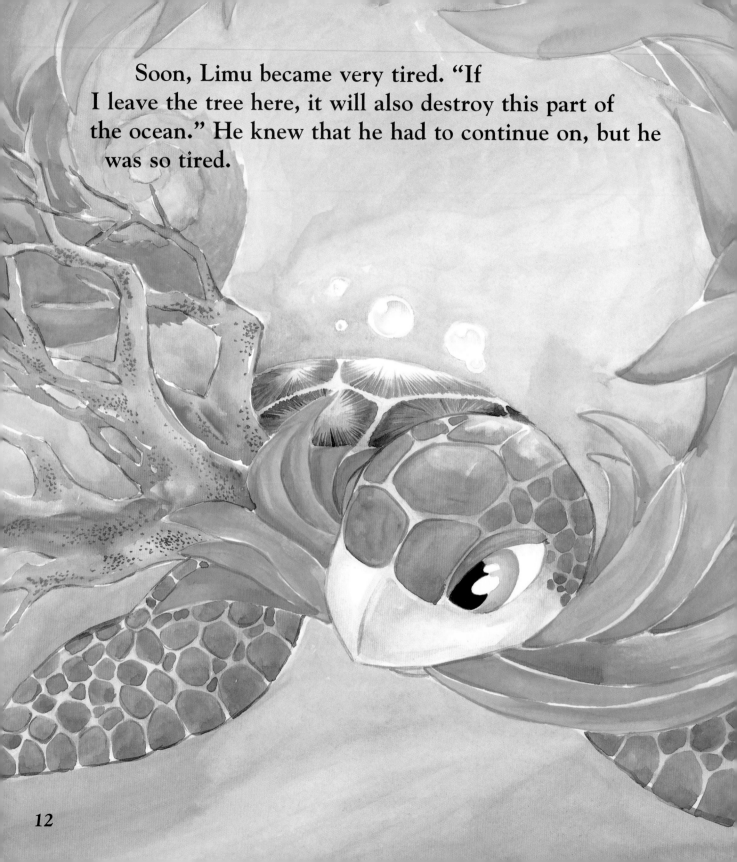

Soon, Limu became very tired. "If
I leave the tree here, it will also destroy this part of
the ocean." He knew that he had to continue on, but he
was so tired.

"You look so silly!" said a voice from the dark blue water. "What are you doing?"

When Limu looked up, he saw a PINK turtle! "You're pink," said Limu.

"Yes, I am, and I am the most beautiful pink turtle in the world! My name is Coral," said the beautiful pink turtle. "What are you doing?" she asked.

"I need to take this tree back to the Faraway-Forest. It is too big and blocks the sunlight from my other ocean plants, and they cannot grow," said Limu.

"My friends and I will help you move it. If you leave the tree here, it might grow in our gardens and destroy our sea plants," said Coral.

"I need your help!" Coral called to her friends.

As Limu looked into the dark blue waters, he saw an army of a hundred jellyfish coming towards him.

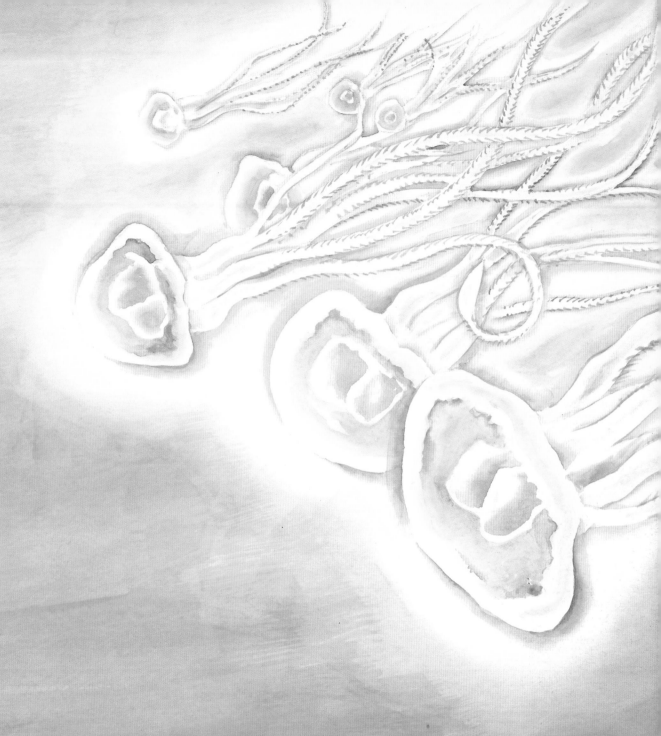

19

They wrapped their long tentacles around the seaweed tree and started swimming towards the Faraway-Forest.

21

Soon they reached a huge forest of seaweed trees. "There must be a million seaweed trees. This is your real home," Limu told the seaweed tree. He replanted the huge tree next to the other trees.

"Thank you," said Limu. "Now, I have to go home and fix my garden. I don't know whether I can do that by myself."

"I will help you," said Coral. "Everyone needs healthy plants to live."

They worked hard to fix his underwater garden.

Some of the seaweeds and fishes never came back, but some did! Their return made all the difference in the world.

Limu and Coral settled down together and enjoyed their new underwater Hawaiian garden...

...with their children, and each child did his or her part to take care of the Hawaiian garden.

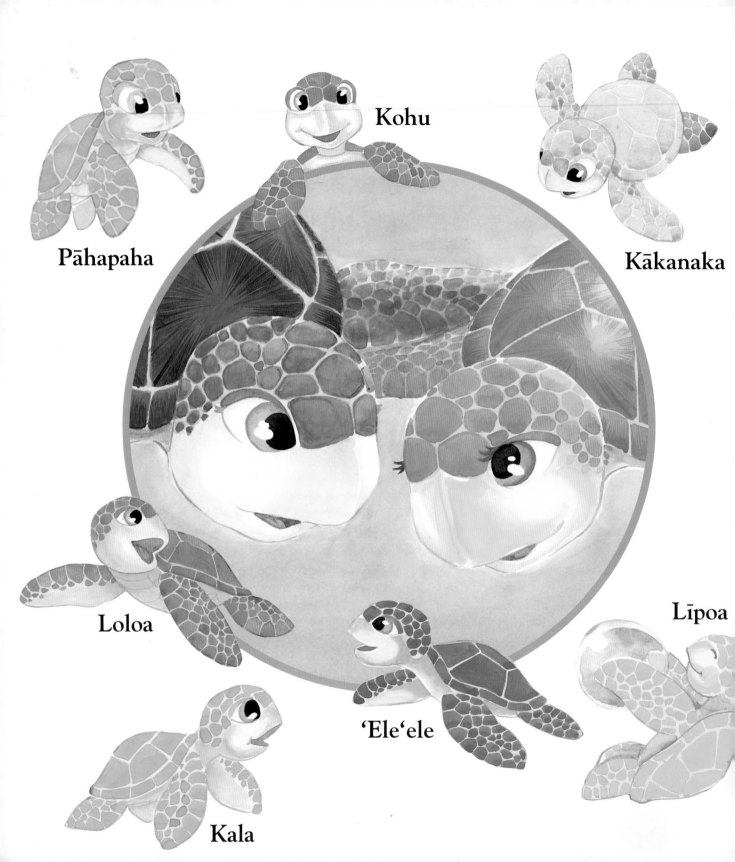

Pāhapaha

Kohu

Kākanaka

Loloa

'Ele'ele

Līpoa

Kala